To Marla,
Enjoy your "garden."

Gary Bower
2012

From Pa & Gram.

The Garden Where I Grow

...and Other Poems for Cultivating a Happy Family

by Gary Bower

Illustrated by Jan Bower

Storybook Meadow Publishing Company
Traverse City, Michigan
www.STORYBOOKMEADOW.com

For our dear grandchildren,

Allyson, Thatcher, Preston, Avree, Lucy, Maylin, Inga, Bella, Destry, Daisy, and Evelyn

Special thanks to our friends and loved ones whose cheery faces appear in these illustrations:

Julia Arbogast	Maylin Bower	Jackson Duggar	Eric Ludy	Glori Mae Rausch
Micah Arbogast	Allyson Breitmeyer	Johannah Duggar	Harper Ludy	Anders Roe
Gavin Bower	Brenda Breitmeyer	Inga Korson	Hudson Ludy	Avree Scott
Grady Bower	Ed Breitmeyer	Isaiah Korson	Kipling Ludy	Shiloh Shaw
Jasmine Bower	Preston Breitmeyer	Tabitha Korson	Leslie Ludy	Ana Sztykiel
Jennifer Bower	Brayden Davis	Avonlea Ludy	Gabriel Norris	John Sztykiel
Kassidy Bower				Lydia Tebben
				Taylor Tebben

The Garden Where I Grow
...and Other Poems for Cultivating a Happy Family

ISBN: 978-0-9845236-2-6
Cover and interior design by Gary Bower
Printed and bound in Canada

The Garden Where I Grow

I watched my Daddy till the ground, turning rocks and weeds.
I helped as Mother staked the rows where we would plant our seeds.
We hoed and raked until we ached, one row, then two, then three.
And when we'd planted several rows, this thought occurred to me:
I was planted somewhere, too – a special garden row.
My roots are in my family, and that is where I grow.
A loving Master Gardener selected just the spot
to sow a seed of love into a fertile garden plot.
He knew just when to plant me, the day, the month, the year.
Of all the families He could choose, He chose to plant me here.
So here is where I'll be content; and one day, time will show
what good may come and blossom from this garden where I grow.

Sunshine and Water

When Daddy loves Mommy in kind, thoughtful ways,
we children are warmed by the wonderful rays
that shine from her heart and beam from her face.
When Daddy loves Mommy, it brightens the place.

When Mommy loves Daddy and shows him respect,
it stirs up a cool and refreshing effect.
We're showered with laughs and a lighthearted wink.
When Mommy loves Daddy we all get a drink.

As sunshine and water come down from the sky,
the love children learn also starts from up high.
So shower and shine for your son and your daughter.
A family will flourish with sunshine and water.

*"...each man must love his wife as he loves himself,
and the wife must respect her husband."*
~ Ephesians 5:33 (NLT)

"Harmony is as refreshing as the dew..."
~ Psalm 133:3 (NLT)

Picking On or Picking With?

Must siblings pick on siblings?
Are family friends a myth?
No one wins by picking on.
They do by picking with.
What a great improvement
by an altered preposition!
We let cooperation rule
instead of competition.
Praise, don't boss, your brother.
Be his biggest fan.
Cheer him on and watch a boy
try hard to be a man.
Help, don't tease, your sister.
Get in "servant mode."
Join your forces as a team
and lighten up the load.
Siblings can be teammates.
No, it's not a myth.
You've tried and failed by picking on.
You'll win by picking with.

*"Dear children, let's not merely say that we love each other;
let us show the truth by our actions."*
~ 1 John 3:18 (NLT)

The Real Pests

In our family garden, we have a pest or two.
No, they aren't my siblings, despite the things they do.
In fact, you just might be surprised;
some things that creep and crawl
are really beneficial and don't harm the plants at all.
Kids can be like earthworms, helpful to a garden.
They work the soil of the heart and help it not to harden.
But plants can be devoured by some other nasty bugs.
Be on the watch for aphids, beetles, grubs, and slugs.

What foes attack a family? Here's a simple guide:
Beware of pests like pettiness, selfishness, and pride.
Watch out for unforgiveness, and careless accusations.
The smallest hint of jealousy can damage good relations.
Tattling and calling names will have a bad effect.
Yelling, whining, undermining; these show disrespect.
We want to have a bumper crop, so I will do my best
to watch and pray and do away with every harmful pest.

*"Get rid of all
bitterness, rage,
and anger..."*

~ Ephesians 4:31 (NIV)

*"Be done with all deceit,
hypocrisy, jealousy, and
all unkind speech."*

~ 1 Peter 2:1 (NLT)

Grandma and Me

I think there's a link
between Grandma and me.
It's hard to explain,
but it's easy to see.
Go ahead; ask her.
I know she'll agree.
There's some kind of bond
between Grandma and me.

We're good for each other,
that is for sure.
I help her with chores.
She helps me mature.
We love and accept
unconditionally.
I'll bet that's the bond
between Grandma and me!

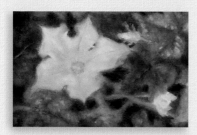

"Grandchildren are the crowning
glory of the aged..."
~ Proverbs 17:6 (NLT)

Grandpa Knows

Who knows how to plant a seed?
Fix a tractor? Pull a weed?
Scare the crows?
Unkink the hose?
These are things that
Grandpa knows.

Who knows how a swing is hung?
How and when to bite his tongue?
Who knows how a mower mows?
Pay attention.
Grandpa knows.

Grandpa's seen the years go by.
Ate his share of humble pie.
Life has taught him, and it shows.
The wise will heed what
Grandpa knows.

"Is not wisdom found among the aged?
Does not long life bring understanding?"

~ Job 12:12 (NIV)

I Know What Gardening Means

About many things I may not know beans.
But gardening? Yes sir, I know what that means.
Everyday hoeing, watering, weeding.
Then comes tomorrow; it all needs repeating.
Later, there's picking, and freezing, and canning.
(Did all this hard work figure into your planning?)
A little neglect can affect the whole crop.
The chores can seem endless. When do they stop?
When all of the harvest is finally in,
our efforts pay off and the feasts can begin.

In raising a family, hard work is required.
When doing it right, you are probably tired.
Tend to it daily. Water with prayer.
Weed them and feed them. Be eager to share
each problem and fear, each deeply felt dream.
Eat meals together. Do chores as a team.
The blisters and back aches may last for a while.
But trust me, your crop will bring more than a smile.
About many things I may not know beans.
But family? Yes sir, I know what that means.

*"You shall teach
(my commands) diligently
to your children..."*

~ Deuteronomy 6:7 (NKJV)

*"Know the state of your flocks,
and put your heart into
caring for your herds..."*

~ Proverbs 27:23 (NLT)

Hidden Among the Thorns

Today I'm picking berries; Mom is baking pies.
I only need a basket and my two observant eyes.
At first, I'm puzzled by how few our bushes are providing.
Then, beneath the leaves I see that many more are hiding.
I slowly comb the bushes, making sure no gems are missed.
My basket claims them all, except a few I can't resist.
As I pick, I feel the prick of thorns among the berries.
It's one of berry picking's little nasty corollaries.
For berries often come with thorns, a tiny price to pay
compared with all the sweet rewards of berry picking day.

Family life, in many ways, is much like picking berries.
We may get pricked, but also, we're the beneficiaries.
Every person has his thorns, but juicy berries, too,
delectable and luscious. Are they hidden from your view?
Walk among the rows and pray for more observant eyes.
Then bring your basket to the Lord.
He'll bake some scrumptious pies.

*"Be patient with each other,
making allowance for
each other's faults..."*

~ Ephesians 4:2 (NLT)

*"...the Holy Spirit produces
this kind of fruit in our lives:
love, joy, peace, patience,
kindness, goodness,
faithfulness, gentleness,
and self-control."*

~ Galatians 5:22-23

Buried Love

Am I growing into someone that my family is enjoying?
Do I do my best to bless them? Can I be a bit annoying?
Are those I care about the most the ones I often hurt?
Does tenderness I feel inside stay buried in my dirt?
Underneath the surface, I feel caring, warm, and loyal.
But no one gains if love remains concealed beneath the soil.
I wonder if my family knows that love has taken root?
What a waste if they can't taste its sweet, nutritious fruit!
Now's as good as anytime to show what's in my heart—
healthy stuff, at least enough to fill a grocery cart!

"Love each other deeply with all your heart."
~ 1 Peter 1:22 (NLT)

Parent Patience

From seed, to sprout, to sturdy stalk, it slowly grows in height.
In time, our corn will reach the sky, but never overnight.
It seems to take forever for corn to grow mature.
I'll bet my parents feel that way...at least, I'm pretty sure.
Because they care, they hang in there and love me all the more.
In time, they'll see produced in me a crop worth waiting for.

"And let us not grow weary while doing good, for in due season we shall reap if we do not lose heart."
~ Galatians 6:9 (NKJV)

Wealthy Family

We never drink from crystal.
Steak is rarely on our platter.
But we're a wealthy family.
We're rich in things that matter.
We love to share our pleasant meals
where jokes are often told.
Laughter is our silver.
Gladness is our gold.
Though steak's not on the menu,
and our tablecloth looks worn,
our spirits feast like merry kings.
We serve a lot of corn.

"...the cheerful heart has a continual feast. Better a little
with the fear of the Lord than great wealth with turmoil.
Better a meal of vegetables where there is love
than a fattened calf with hatred."
~ Proverbs 15:15-17 (NIV)

19

Baby Now

One day at Mommy's checkup, the doctor said to me,
"Someday a little baby's going to join your family tree."
I puzzled at the doctor's comment as we drove away.
A little baby someday? Then what is it today?

Later, in our melon patch, it all made perfect sense.
All around me at my feet I saw clear evidence.
I saw how watermelons grew while clinging to the vine.
Everywhere I looked I saw a similar design.
A melon stays connected to its parent as it grows,
and yet, it's still a melon, as everybody knows.
And if it's true for watermelons, pumpkins, peas, and corn,
then babies must be people long before they're even born.
Oh sure, they're small and fragile, not fully ripened yet,
but just as human and alive as human beings get.

Today I hugged my Mommy's tummy
and I whispered, "Wow!
You're not a Baby Someday.
You're our Baby Now."

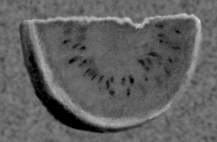

"Before I formed you in
the womb, I knew you;
before you were born
I set you apart..."
~ Jeremiah 1:5
(NIV)

"You knit me together
in my mother's womb.
I will praise you because
I am fearfully and
wonderfully made.."
~ Psalm 139:13-14
(NIV)

Sharing a Garden

There once was a time as I started to grow
that I was the feature; the star of the show.
Back in that season, I didn't know
I'd be sharing this garden with you.

Praises were poured on my cute little head.
"Oh, what a dear!" my admirers said.
Lately, attention goes elsewhere instead.
Have I ceded my garden to you?

But I am not hanging my head in defeat.
Having a sibling can be kind of sweet.
I want to enjoy you instead of compete,
and grow in this garden with you.

You're not just some rival I need to outdo.
I choose a happier, healthier view.
I'll teach you some new things like tying your shoe,
exploring this garden with you.

Sometimes I wonder, who's learning from whom?
We help each other to blossom and bloom.
There's much to discover, and plenty of room
to thrive in this garden with you.

"And he has given us this
command: Anyone who
loves God must also love
their brother and sister."
~ 1 John 4:21 (NIV)

"Dear brothers and sisters...we
are thankful that your faith is
flourishing and you are all
growing in love for each other."
~ 2 Thessalonians 1:3 (NLT)

Refreshing Relatives

At times, we face a hot spell that is dusty, dull, and dry.
Hearts and hope can wither underneath a cloudless sky.
Before our leaves begin to wilt, before our spirits sink,
the Master Gardener provides a cool, refreshing drink.
And how does He give moisture to His weary, thirsty plants?
Often through extended family -- cousins, uncles, aunts.
An understanding in-law may be just the tool He uses.
Perhaps a nephew or a niece will be the one He chooses.
Yes, caring relatives are folks that everybody needs.
They lend a hand. They lend an ear.
They do some thoughtful deeds.
No matter where you sink your roots,
or where your family lives,
I hope you keep in contact with
refreshing relatives.

"May the Lord make your love increase and overflow for each other..."
~ 1 Thessalonians 3:12 (NIV)

"Let the smile of your face shine on us, Lord.
You have given me greater joy than those who
have abundant harvests of grain and wine."
~ Psalm 4:6-7 (NLT)

"Those who plant in tears will
harvest with shouts of joy."
~ Psalm 126:5 (NLT)

Mother's Eyes

What is that in Mother's eyes?
I've seen it now and then.
It flashes like a fast surprise.
There it is again!

Now I'm very curious.
Whatever could it be?
It sparkles so. Hey, I know...
It's her delight in me!

Outlasting Love

Every hope and every doubt; every storm and every frost;
Every insect, every drought; every crop that's ever lost;
Every planting in the spring; every harvest in the fall;
Every turn that life may bring –
A farmer must outlast them all.

Every cough and every cry; every fuss and every fright;
Every whimper, every "why?"; every single sleepless night;
Every time her child strays; every failure, every fall;
Every attitude and phase –
A mother's love outlasts them all.

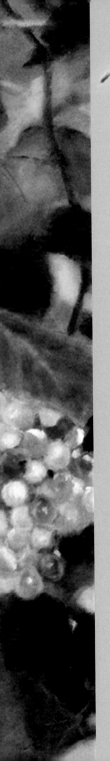

"We will not hide these truths from our children;
we will tell the next generation
about the glorious deeds of the Lord...
He commanded our ancestors
to teach them to their children...
and they in turn will teach their own children.
So each generation should set its hope anew on Go[d]
not forgetting his glorious miracles
and obeying his commands."

~ Psalm 78:4-7 (NLT)

"How joyful are those who fear the Lord
and delight in obeying his commands.
Their children will be successful everywhere;
an entire generation of godly
people will be blessed."

~ Psalm 112:1-2 (NLT)